D0174779

Christian Jr./Sr High School
2100 Greenfield Dr
El Cajon, CA 92019

one small

Miracle

one small

Miracle

T 14902

Lance Wubbels

Christian Jr./Sr High School
2100 Greenfield Dr
El Cajon, CA 92019

BETHANY HOUSE PUBLISHERS
MINNEAPOLIS, MINNESOTA 55438

All scripture quotations, unless indicated, are taken from the HOLY BIBLE, NEW INTERNATIONAL VERSION®. Copyright © 1973, 1978, 1984 by International Bible Society. Used by permission of Zondervan Publishing House. All rights reserved. The "NIV" and "New International Version" Trademarks are registered in the United States Patent and Trademark Office by International Bible Society. Use of either trademark requires the permission of International Bible Society.

Cover illustration by Jennifer Heyd Wharton.
Book insides designed by Sherry Paavola.

Published by Bethany House Publishers
A Ministry of Bethany Fellowship, Inc.
11300 Hampshire Avenue South, Minneapolis, Minnesota 55438

Printed in the United States of America

Library of Congress Cataloging-in-Publication Data
Wubbels, Lance
    One small miracle / Lance Wubbels.
        p.   cm.
    ISBN 1-55661-668-6 (hardcover)
    1. Teacher-student relationships—United States—Fiction.
2. Elementary school teachers—United States—Fiction.
3. Women teachers—United States—Fiction.
4. Girls—United States—Fiction.   I. Title
PS3573.U3905 1995   95—480
813'.54—dc20   CIP

To
Gary & Carol Johnson

I'm not sure what you saw,
how you knew,
or why you believed,
but there's no doubt
that this small book
and all of the other books
are deeply rooted in you.
I cannot thank you enough.

LANCE WUBBELS, the Managing
Editor of Bethany House Publishers, taught
biblical studies courses at Bethany College
of Missions for many years. He is the author
of the World War II fiction series, The
Gentle Hills, with Bethany House. He is
also the compiler and editor of the Charles
Spurgeon and F. B. Meyer Christian Living
Classic books with Emerald Books.

THE GENTLE HILLS

Far From the Dream
Whispers in the Valley
Keeper of the Harvest

(All available in large print.)

Let us not become weary in doing good,
for at the proper time we will reap a harvest if we do
not give up. Therefore, as we have opportunity,
let us do good to all people, especially to those
who belong to the family of believers.

Galatians 6:9–10

Confident that her day was well planned, Sophie Lawson sat at her neatly arranged desk silently observing her incoming class of sixth-grade boys and girls. To her own amazement, twelve years of teaching had done nothing to diminish her anticipation of the first morning's class. Like some of the children already settled in their desks, Sophie had slept little the previous night, her sleep having fled before the exciting possibilities of the year to come. Just the thought of a new group of eager students guaranteed her a fitful night of tossing and turning.

With the true heart of a teacher, Sophie gazed from one young face to another, trying to assess each life entrusted into her care. As had been true of every new class she welcomed into her room, the atmosphere was abuzz with excitement as the students squeezed out the last fleeting seconds of

summer before the classroom bell rang another
school year into session.

Most of the faces were very familiar to Sophie.
Having moved with her husband to the small rural
town of Harmony after college graduation, Sophie
had gotten to know most of the families in the community. She had taught many older brothers and
sisters of these children here today. Sophie's trained
eye could easily spot the brightest and best students,
the class clown, the popular ones, the shy ones, and
the extroverts. But the children most obvious to her
were the "damaged" ones. Every year, her list seemed
to grow longer and longer as more children arrived
having been damaged by divorce, abuse, lack of love,
or neglect.

Her searching gaze reached the middle of the
third row and rested on the only new girl in the
classroom. Mary Bartel had moved to Harmony in
late August to live with her grandmother after living
with her aunt for a short time. In contrast to the
bright colors and stylish designs worn by the stu-

dents around her, Mary wore a faded cotton print dress that hung down below her knees but failed to cover her tattered pink tennis shoes. Her long, straight brown hair was parted in the middle and carried the dull, telltale appearance of not having been washed in recent days. Mary's flat-white face was expressionless as she stared absently out the classroom window.

With a slight shake of her head and a deep sigh, Sophie covered her lips with her hand and whispered to herself, "Oh, my. What am I going to do with her?" From reviewing the available records, Sophie was aware of Mary's difficult background, but she had hoped Mary's physical appearance would not prove such a perfect match. As much as she hated it, Sophie could not restrain the thought that every year she had had at least one child who seemed beyond the hope of helping, and this year Mary Bartel looked the part.

The fact was, Sophie Lawson already knew a good deal about Mary, and seeing her now only

confirmed that knowledge. Because Mary's move to
Harmony had been so close to the beginning of the
school year, her records from the previous elementary school had not yet arrived. But Sophie had
called Mary's school and asked the administrator to
fax whatever information she thought would be
important. The fax read:

*I wish I had better news to report on Mary Bartel.
She is perceived to be a bright girl, but is very reserved
and very slow. When Mary was three, her father aban-
doned both her and her mother, and never returned. She
has no friends and appears to enjoy being a loner.*

*Mary often daydreams in the classroom and is not
achieving her potential. She seems to receive little or no
help at home, and occasionally comes to class angry and
sullen after having been left alone while her mother
worked or socialized at the bar.*

*She is extremely unmotivated, answers questions in
monosyllables, and does just enough schoolwork to get
by. Her hair is seldom combed and her clothes smell
musty. During Mary's third-grade year, her mother's*

boyfriend came to live with them, and according to police
reports, they fought all the time.

Mary's mother was diagnosed with lung cancer and
her health failed quickly during Mary's fourth-grade year.
That illness stretched into the following year and caused
Mary to struggle even more to keep up. She was nearly
held back at the midyear point. Her mother died in the
spring, and Mary was taken in by her mother's sister,
who seems to regard Mary as a burden.

Sophie's gaze moved across the other half of the
room, but her heart was still on Mary. The dreaded
words trudged slowly through her mind: *unmotivated,
daydreamer, slow, a burden. Every year there is at least
one who drags—*

The ringing of the
classroom bell
broke through her
reverie, and a sud-
den burst of adrenaline
cleared away the dark,
somber reflections.

Sophie took a deep breath and smiled, picked up her student list, then stood to greet her class.

"Good morning, class," she spoke warmly, stepping forward and looking around the room into the bright, cheery faces looking attentively at her. "My name is Mrs. Lawson, and I would like to welcome you to the sixth grade. Is anyone here this morning who's not in the sixth grade?"

A slight ripple of confusion broke over the class, and Sophie looked quickly down into the bewildered face of a known troublemaker.

"Curtis Shepherd," she said firmly. "You are eleven years old and a member of the Harmony sixth-grade class, correct?"

"Yes, ma'am," Curtis mumbled, quickly sitting up straight in his chair.

"Yes, Mrs. Lawson," Sophie corrected him.

Curtis's eyes grew large, and he gulped. "Yes, Mrs. Lawson."

Sophie nodded and smiled. "Just testing you, Curtis. You passed."

Puffing a sigh of relief and shaking his head, Curtis whispered a "phew" through a big grin. Soft laughter filled the room, and the children relaxed.

"Now," declared Sophie, crossing her arms and getting down to business, "I want you to know that along with learning a great deal this year, we're also going to have a lot of fun. I have studied each of your student files and am very excited to have such a fine group as you. But you need to know that I am in charge, and I suggest you not challenge whether I back that up with discipline. My intention is to make learning a fun experience for you, but if you choose to make it difficult, I can make it difficult as well. Understood?"

Nodding heads signaled that the point had been taken to heart.

"Good," she continued. "I'm going to take roll, and when I read your name, I'd like you to stand and briefly tell us something fun you did this summer."

Sophie looked down at her alphabetical list and called, "Ginny Anderson."

A pixy little girl with curly auburn hair jumped up and took only a few seconds to gather her thoughts. "I flew to Seattle and spent two whole weeks with my cousins," she announced. "And I rode on the airplane by myself!"

As Ginny took her seat, Sophie commented, "That was brave of you. Were you afraid?"

"Just a little," Ginny answered with a nervous giggle.

"We're proud of you," Sophie affirmed, giving Ginny a wink. "Part of learning is being brave enough to try something new. And we're going to have many new things to try this year, so let's learn from Ginny's flying to Seattle by herself."

Looking down at her sheet, Sophie gave a silent moan and turned her attention to the plain girl sitting in the third row. "We have a brand-new student in our class this year, and I'd like to introduce to you all our new friend, Mary Bartel."

Without speaking or smiling, Mary stood up slowly and stared into Sophie's face.

For the first time, Sophie noticed her almond-shaped brown eyes and her beautiful long lashes. *She's like a wounded little bird, yet so pretty*, Sophie thought, gazing into her new student's inscrutable face.

Mary stood motionless, and the class waited uneasily as she blankly stared at her teacher.

"Mary, welcome to my class," Sophie said with a reassuring smile. "Can you tell us something you did this summer that was fun?"

A momentary frown flitted across Mary's forehead, and she squinted her eyes in thought. "No, ma'am—Mrs. Lawson," she answered finally.

Caught off guard by the response, Sophie paused while some of the children began to snicker. "Why can't you tell us, Mary?" she asked.

"Because I can't think of anything that happened this summer that was fun," Mary said hollowly, gazing at Sophie with haunted eyes.

Dear God, Sophie groaned inwardly as Mary sat down, and the class fell into a stunned silence.

The King will reply,
"I tell you the truth, whatever you
did for one of the least of these
brothers of mine, you did for me."
Matthew 25:40

"So, is it going any better with Mary?" Sophie's husband Bill asked as they drove toward school on a frosty Minnesota morning just a few days before Halloween. "Were you able to get her grandmother to help?"

"Not much," replied Sophie with a cold shiver. "She works long days at the rest home and seems to be too tired to care. She said she'd try, but Mary's still coming to school with dirty hair, wearing one of her two ugly dresses. None of the kids can stand to be around her—she smells."

"What's Harold got to say about it?"

"He gives me the same 'principal' advice he gives you for your third graders," Sophie sputtered. "Care to guess? You've heard it several times yourself."

"Do the *best* you can with what you've *got*," Bill mimicked Harold Dickson's intonations perfectly.

"Very good," Sophie replied. "And he said to do

all I could to help her with her bookwork. But, of course, Mary's not quite needy enough to qualify for special help."

"Of course," Bill nodded, turning into the school parking lot. "Right through the cracks she goes."

"Exactly," lamented Sophie. "It's the one thing I hate about teaching. Sometimes I wonder if I've stopped caring."

Bill Lawson pulled into a parking spot and turned off the car engine. "You're too hard on yourself, Sophie," he reminded her for the hundredth time. "Remember that you've got twenty-five kids to help. You can't let Mary hold the other children back."

"You're plagiarizing lines from Harold again, aren't you?" teased Sophie, looking into her husband's dark brown eyes. "You'll make a good principal when he retires. But seriously, no matter how much time I'd like to give Mary, the twenty-four others make sure it won't happen. I've got all I can do to keep up with them."

"That's life, honey," Bill whispered, leaning over

to give Sophie a kiss before saying goodbye for the day. "Oh, what about the music concert tonight? Are you going home beforehand?"

"No, there's not enough time," she replied. "I have to make paper sailor hats for my class to wear while they sing tonight. I am worried about the concert, though. Did I tell you that Warren asked Mary to sing a solo?"

"What?"

"He's discovered that Mary has a lovely voice, while the rest of the class sound like a chorus of frogs. He was desperate and decided to chance it with Mary."

"Oh, boy," Bill muttered, shaking his head and lifting his briefcase from the backseat. "Glad you warned me. I'll be praying all day."

"Please do," Sophie urged, pushing her car door open and letting in a gust of cold air. "If it goes well, it could be a big step for her. But if it goes poorly..."

As Sophie walked silently toward her classroom, she prayed first for Mary and then for herself.

Although she made a conscious effort to love all her students the same, Sophie was aware of her own shortcomings. There were the times when she felt good about marking incorrect answers on tests and giving low grades to those she thought deserved them. There was also the occasional fudging for the students she really enjoyed most. And despite how hard she tried, there was the giving in to weariness when trying to help students like Mary, especially when no sign of thanks was forthcoming.

The day sped by quickly, and after correcting the day's tests, Sophie found she barely had time to finish making the paper sailor hats before the children began to arrive for the concert. One by one they marched into the room, all dressed up and ready to go.

It was just shortly before they were to leave for the gymnasium that Mary finally walked through the door and headed for her seat. To everyone's surprise, she was wearing a lovely white blouse with a black skirt and new shoes; even her hair had been washed and gleamed with a healthy shine. For a moment, the classroom quieted, then quickly the children returned to their chatter and disregarded Mary.

Sophie looked at a strikingly pretty Mary and wondered what her life might have been like had she been fortunate enough to grow up in a healthy family. She thought she caught the beginning of a smile on Mary's face when she took her seat. *Strange*, she thought, *two months and I don't recall her ever smiling.*

Looking down at her watch, Sophie noted it was time to go. She stood and told the children to walk in single file to the gymnasium and take their assigned seats. As they exited the classroom, Sophie passed out the paper sailor hats, waiting to give Mary a special captain's hat because of her solo part.

"This is just for you, Mary," Sophie whispered, handing her the long black captain's hat, held together with gold yarn. "You look wonderful. I hope it goes well for you."

Mary stopped and broke into a wide grin at the

sight of the hat. "For me, Mrs. Lawson?" she gasped, taking the paper hat gently into her hands. Her delicate features lit up and her eyes sparkled as she looked into her teacher's kind face.

"Yes, for you," Sophie replied, putting her hand on Mary's shoulder. "But don't put it on until you get to the platform. We don't want you to mess your lovely hair."

Escorting Mary down the hallway, Sophie and her class took their seats in the small, crowded gymnasium and awaited their turn. Sophie watched Mary for any signs of nervousness, but the familiar blank cloud had settled upon her face again, hiding any emotion that might be rising toward the surface.

Finally, after what had already seemed to be a long program, Mrs. Lawson's sixth-grade class rose to their feet and headed for the platform. As the students reached the stage, they pulled their paper sailor caps open and put them on. Mary was last, and after placing her captain's cap on her head, she stepped to the front where the music director had shown her to stand.

Sophie held her breath, and suddenly nervous tremors began to ripple through her body. Despite the special hat, Mary looked more like a little lamb than like a proud sea captain. Waves of panic overcame her as she realized she should have intervened and prevented Warren from giving Mary the solo part. The risk of damage was too great.

With the class finally in position and all the hats straightened, Warren Finley nodded to the pianist, who began playing through the melody. It was a silly song, and Sophie wondered why Warren had picked it. Mary was to begin the first line: "Cape Cod girls, they have no combs, heave away, heave away. They comb their hair with codfish bones, we are bound for Australia." Then the rest of the class was to join in the equally silly refrain.

As the preliminary melody ended, Warren nodded to Mary, who stepped forward and opened her mouth to sing, but nothing came out. Warren quickly raised his hand, and the woman stopped playing the piano.

"Clear your throat!" whispered Warren as a murmur began to fill the gymnasium.

Mary rattled her throat and gave a hum.

The director nodded toward the accompanist, who replayed the melody, and the crowd again focused its attention upon Mary. With the motion of his hands and an extra large smile, Warren pointed to Mary, who once again opened her mouth. This time, nothing escaped but a tiny whisper.

Warren raised his hand, and as the piano went silent, the gymnasium quickly filled with a roar of laughter. A sea of faces, both in front and back of Mary, broke into a sickening hilarity that left Sophie stunned and angry. Looking at the parents seated near her, whose faces had taken on the look of hyenas, Sophie found herself rising to her feet in outrage.

As she stepped out into the aisle and raised her hands, the gymnasium quieted as quickly as it had become raucous. "I am amazed that you find so much humor in this," Sophie declared with bold indignation. "Mary came to sing for you tonight, and I think you owe her enough respect to be quiet until she finishes."

A shameful and embarrassed pall settled over many adult faces, and Sophie slowly turned back toward the platform. "Mary," she urged, "try one more time, sweetheart. It's okay if you can't do it, but will you try once more, for me?"

Mary nodded shyly, and pushing her captain's hat back up into position, she fixed her soft brown eyes upon her teacher. Sophie remained standing in the aisle, and as the melody began for the third time, tears began to flow down her cheeks.

Opening her mouth this time, Mary somehow found her lovely singing voice, and nearly broke into a smile as she led her class through four silly verses of a song that no one in the gymnasium that day would ever forget.

*Dear children, let us not love with words or tongue
but with actions and in truth.
This then is how we know that we belong to the truth,
and how we set our hearts at rest in his presence,*

1 John 3:18–19

hen she failed the second time and everyone started laughing, I turned around and saw the fire in your eyes," Bill Lawson remarked as he crawled into bed later that night. "I knew you were coming up out of that chair, but I had no idea what you were going to do."

"Neither did I, let me assure you," Sophie responded, replaying the scene in her mind and feeling the rush of anger again. "I've never been so upset before. Ropes wouldn't have stopped me."

"That little girl sang for you, you know," Bill reasoned. "Did you see the look in her eyes?"

"Only partially," answered Sophie, giving a sigh and trying to relax. "I was crying so hard I couldn't see much."

"She was incredible, and so were you," said Bill, arranging his pillow just the way he liked it. "I was so proud of you I felt like cheering."

Sophie laughed and rolled over toward Bill. "Do you think I went too far?"

"Come again?"

"Do you think I failed to act like a teacher?" Sophie asked seriously. "Was I was out of control?"

"You're serious?"

"Very," Sophie continued. "I feel like I did what I had to do, but it's like nothing I've ever done before. I'm supposed to be a professional—cool, calm, rational. Did I go too far?"

"You stood up to protect your student from something that could have hurt her for the rest of her life, Sophie," Bill reassured her. "Just because you've never been pushed this far before doesn't make your response wrong. Maybe you're just being stretched."

"What?"

"I don't know," Bill mumbled. "It's too late, and I'm too tired. Let's talk about it tomorrow."

"You won't be sleeping until you explain what

you meant," warned Sophie.

Bill yawned. "I really didn't mean much of anything. I just wonder if you're being stretched in your role as a teacher, that's all. What you're feeling is different, but it's probably good. Get it?"

"I'm not sure."

"Think about it and tell me what you come up with in the morning." Bill groaned and rolled over.

Sophie never ceased to be amazed at how quickly her husband could drop off to sleep. So many nights while he was merrily snoring away, she lay wide awake beside him, staring up at the ceiling. This night was no exception.

She churned the incident over and over in her mind, but kept coming back to the underlying feeling that something still wasn't quite right, that somehow she hadn't done enough. And that upset her, because she couldn't imagine what more she could have done.

Despite how long it took Sophie to fall asleep that night, the next morning she awoke in typical fashion just seconds before the alarm went off. Bill was still sleeping, so she turned the alarm off and decided to let him get a few extra minutes' sleep. As she pulled her hand from the clock, Sophie suddenly recalled the dream she had had just before waking.

The dream had been very short but was exceptionally vivid. Sophie clearly saw Mary standing before her in the classroom, looking as sad and unappealing as on the first morning of school. She was speaking to Mary just four simple words: "Mary, I love you." And that was the end of the dream.

Strange, Sophie thought. *Why would I be...?*

That was all the wondering she needed to do. The meaning of the dream couldn't be more clear if it had been written on the wall. She was not to be merely the best teacher she could be. Indeed, there was something more. She was to be a messenger of God's love for all children, especially for the Marys who would walk into her life year after year. She was to give herself to loving her children, and to doing for them those things that would meet their special

needs, despite the personal cost. And she was to stop
believing there were children so damaged she could
not make a difference in their lives.

Sophie rose quietly and walked across the bed-
room to the large window facing east. A thin line
of red was painting its way across the dark blue
horizon, extending the promise of a lovely autumn
day. The fading twinkle of morning stars signaled
the departing of night.

"Father," Sophie whispered, "put Your love for
children inside me. My best love falls so short of
what they need, especially what the slow ones like
Mary need. Jesus, change me to be like You. Do
whatever it takes to make me like You."

Standing at the window for several minutes,
Sophie let the dream rerun its simple message of
truth again and again. She could sense a strengthen-
ing of resolve in her heart to be a different teacher,
a new teacher every day by the grace of God. And
Sophie knew it began with Mary.

To the untrained eye, school that day at

Harmony Elementary looked like any other day. But for several boys and girls in Mrs. Lawson's sixth-grade class, it was truly a new day. In ways both small and large, they found their teacher suddenly aware of their individual needs, and aggressively pursuing the reasons they were not understanding their school-work. It may have been the gentle touch on a shoulder or the sitting down with them during a break, but they could mark the morning when "everything changed."

As the last bell rang for the day and her students were dashing for the door, Sophie stopped Mary and asked her to stay for a few minutes. Mary looked up wide-eyed but nodded.

"Did I do something wrong, Mrs. Lawson?" asked Mary as the last student exited the classroom. "I'm sorry I did so poorly on the math quiz."

"No, no. It's not about the quiz or anything you've done, Mary," Sophie answered soothingly and pointed to the brown metal chair by her desk. "Please sit down. I've got a few things I need to say."

Seeing Mary return today in her faded old dress and wearing once again her dull expression after having looked so pretty and alive the night before saddened Sophie, and reminded her of the story of Cinderella and the glass slipper. For a moment she hesitated, wondering again if what she had purposed to do was the right thing. But the memory of Mary's smile put a halt to all her doubts.

"Mary, I was very proud of you last night," Sophie began, looking into Mary's brown almond-shaped eyes. "I think it was the bravest thing I've ever seen anyone do. I'm afraid I would have run off the stage if I had been in your shoes."

Mary's face began to warm and a wrin- kled smile broke through. "I want- ed to run, but I was too afraid. I wouldn't have

tried the third time if you hadn't done what you did.
You gave me courage."

Sophie closed her eyes, but closing them could
not stop the onrush of tears. She put one hand over
her face and slowly rocked back and forth as the
tears fell. The amazing sight of Mary singing her silly
song loomed large in Sophie's mind, and with it
came a joy too deep for her to contain.

"I'm sorry, Mrs. Lawson," Mary said softly. "I
didn't mean to—"

Holding up her hand and shaking her head,
Sophie stopped Mary, but still could not speak.
Opening a desk drawer and taking out a handful
of tissues, she dried her tears and took a deep breath.
Sophie had expected this to be difficult, but she
hadn't expected to cry.

"You'll have to forgive me for getting emotional,"
Sophie murmured. "It's hard to explain what's going
on inside me, but what you said made me so happy
that it just came out this way."

Sophie gave a little embarrassed laugh, and for

the first time, Mary laughed as well. It came as such a delightful surprise to Sophie that for a moment she had to simply sit and wait for her feelings to subside before speaking again.

"I'm going to be very brief, but I want you to listen very closely to what I have to say. Okay?" Sophie asked. "I have some things to say that I should have said before, so I need to make sure you understand me now."

Mary nodded, looking perplexed.

Covering her mouth with her hand, Sophie closed her eyes again and prayed for the right words. Then with a sigh, she looked at Mary and took her hand. "As your teacher, I can't do anything about the hurt you felt when your mother died, or about your feelings when your father left you. Nor can I do anything about all the other hardships you've had to face. But I want you to know that I am very sorry, and if I could make it all better, I would. Do you understand that?"

A tear began to form at the corner of Mary's left

eye, and she gave a little shudder. With her eyes fastened on her teacher's, she whispered, "Why?"

Sophie shook her head and gently smiled. "I was afraid you'd ask me that. I'm not sure you'll believe my answer, but will you try?"

Mary nodded again.

"Because I love you, Mary."

The only change of expression on Mary's face was the rapid blinking of her long lashes.

"This is not just about tears, or concern for the past, it's also about today," Sophie explained, squeezing Mary's hand in hers. "I know you're behind the rest of the class in your schoolwork, and I'm here to help you. If you want my help, I'll stay after school every day I can and help you in whatever subject you're struggling. Even your math!"

Mary smiled again, then a giggle slipped out and her face was momentarily transformed. But the shadows returned to her countenance, and Mary said, "Thank you, Mrs. Lawson, but I don't want to waste your time. My mother always told me I was too stupid to learn like other kids."

Sophie shook her head in disbelief, then reached her arms around Mary and hugged her tightly. "It's not true, Mary," she whispered in her ear. "Perhaps your mother was confused or misinformed, but it's simply not true. You don't believe it, do you?"

"No. Not really."

"And if you could catch up to the other kids, you'd like that, right?"

"I'm awfully far behind."

"But you'd like to catch up, wouldn't you?"

"Yes."

"Then let's start on your math right now. Can you stay?"

"Yes."

"Do you need to call your grandmother?"

"No. She's never home till late."

"Well, get your math book, and let's see what we can do."

123

Religion that God our
Father accepts as pure
and faultless is this:
to look after orphans
and widows in their
distress and to keep
oneself from being
polluted by the world.
James 1:27

*I*t wasn't long before several of Mrs. Lawson's students were staying after class for help.

Some were further behind than Sophie had thought, but Mary was far behind the slowest of the pack. Working with Mary in the late afternoons, Sophie wondered how it was possible that Mary was still in the same classroom with children her own age.

Sophie knew the key to helping her students catch up was patience, but she would have gladly paid big dollars for a magic wand to wave over them. Time after time she found herself repeating the basics, thinking they understood, only to discover they didn't, moving a few steps forward, only to fall back again. Progress, when it came, was agonizingly slow.

By Thanksgiving, there was very little measurable evidence that the extra effort was making a difference. Truthfully, there was no evidence at all. But Sophie was certain the foundations being laid would eventually pay off, and by Christmas the signs of breakthroughs were as visible as the budding of trees in springtime. It came to one student at a time, sometimes while working alone and sometimes while working with Sophie. But the light seemed to suddenly click on, and what had baffled each student for so long was finally understood.

On the day of the Christmas party, Sophie could not remember ever having had such a happy group of students. It seemed the joy of accomplishment experienced by some was spreading to others. Even Mary, who still had miles of catching up to do, had found a close friend in Anne Walters and was growing more confident as her classwork improved.

As the students were preparing to leave for vacation, Sophie overheard Anne whispering to another girl, "They don't even have a Christmas tree or any presents in their apartment! Mary's grandmother spends most of her money at the casino."

All the joy and laughter Sophie had so delighted in throughout the day evaporated in an instant. Yet despite the sick feeling in her stomach, Sophie

managed to smile and to wish her students a Merry
Christmas as they joyfully marched out of the classroom for two weeks of freedom from schoolwork. But
once the room was empty, Sophie leaned against the
doorway and stared absently across the classroom.

The sound of familiar footsteps in the hallway
caused Sophie to turn and smile. "You ready to go
already! I haven't even straightened my desk."

"Forget it!" Bill Lawson said, reaching out and
kissing her gently on the cheek. "Let's get out of
here. What are you standing around for?"

Sophie sighed and shook her head, the sickening
feeling washing over her again.

"So was your Christmas party a bomb?"

"No," Sophie replied, walking back to her desk
and putting away some of her opened books. "I
happened to hear Anne Walters tell a friend that
Mary Bartel won't be having a Christmas this year.
No tree or presents. Apparently her grandmother
squanders all her extra money at the casino."

"That surprises you?"

"No. Not the gambling," Sophie said, plopping

down in her chair. "I just hate the thought of Mary going home to an empty apartment and a Christmasless vacation. That's dreadful."

Bill blew out a gust of air and nodded his agreement. Sitting down in the brown metal chair next to Sophie, he said, "I can't imagine it. Christmas at our house was the greatest time of the whole year."

"There must be something we can do."

"Like what?" Bill asked cautiously. "We're leaving tomorrow morning—remember? And we still have to pack. You do—"

"Yes, I remember," Sophie cut in. "We'll be ready, as always. But think about Mary for a minute. What if we could make her Christmas special? What if we..."

Sophie's words drifted off, and the two of them sat quietly in their chairs thinking about what they might do. It didn't take Bill long to come up with an idea.

"Got it!" he said, crossing his arms smugly. "How willing are you to help her?"

"Very."

"Okay, how about this?" Bill asked. "We could give them our artificial tree with all the trimmings."

"It's an expensive—"

"I know what it cost, but we're not even going to be at home to enjoy it. Besides, now that we own our own house, I've been thinking we need a bigger tree. How about if I unplug the lights, pick our little tree up, and take the whole thing over to them just the way it is? I think it'll fit in the back of the van."

Sophie studied her husband closely and asked, "You're serious?"

"Certainly," he said. "You said you wanted to do something special, so let's do something special! Let's do it now!"

Laughing as Bill jumped up and headed for the door, Sophie called out, "Hold on, buster! I've got a couple more ideas. And they won't even take long."

Bill turned and slowly walked back to the desk. "Time's wasting, Sophie. What've you got?"

"Before you go home and get the tree in the van," she said, grinning from ear to ear, "drop me off at the clothing store. I'm going to buy Mary two new school outfits and hope she gets rid of those tacky old dresses. The store will gift wrap them, and we're done. That's simple, eh?"

Bill was smiling, too. "That's a great idea," he assured her. "But what about Mary's grandmother?"

"What about her?"

Shrugging his shoulders, Bill said, "Shouldn't we get her something, too?"

"I wouldn't know—"

"What about food?" asked Bill. "We could give her a small turkey and all the other food to make a Christmas dinner. We pack it up in one big box and put her name on it!"

"Why not?" Sophie jumped out of her chair and gave Bill a big hug. "This is going to be our most fun Christmas ever!"

Later that evening, Sophie and Bill Lawson stood anxiously on the landing outside Mary's apartment door, hoping no one would come out in the hallway and see what they were doing. Bill had lugged up a big box of food and placed it beside the Christmas tree. Under the tree sat three brightly wrapped pre-

sents containing two school outfits and a new pair
of shoes.

"Plug it in!" whispered Sophie, pointing to an
electrical socket beside the hallway door.

Bill laughed quietly as he put the plug into the
socket, lighting up the Christmas tree. "Let's run for
it!" he exclaimed.

Sophie reached up to the doorbell, pushed it, and
together they yelled, "Mary's Christmas!" Dashing
down the stairs and out the apartment building
doors, they raced to their still-running car. Both
were laughing so hard, they could barely catch their
breath once they were in the car.

"Go! Go! Go!" Sophie cried, looking back up at
the second-floor apartment as Bill gunned the
engine and headed out the snow-packed driveway
into the cold darkness.

But to Sophie's surprise, their anonymous escape
was foiled by the solitary figure standing in the frost-
draped window, smiling and waving to them. Little
Mary had caught them in the act.

Give, and it will be given to you.
A good measure, pressed down, shaken together and running over, will be poured into your lap. For with the measure you use, it will be measured to you.
Luke 6:38

Sophie's birthday fell on Valentine's Day, and it had become a class tradition for her students to gather around the large art table to watch as she opened their special gifts. Each year, the classroom filled with laughter and happy "oo's" and "ah's" when the wrappings came off and the gifts were revealed. Although most of the presents were inexpensive or made by the children themselves, as long as Sophie looked pleased, her students were delighted.

This year's class had finished their valentine party and had moved on to the day's bigger event. Stacked high on the art table was a mound of presents for Sophie, all from the boys and girls of her class. Most of the gifts were wrapped in colorful paper, but tucked in the middle of the pile was a plain white bakery sack with big red hearts drawn around the edges and closed at the top with cheap red tape cut in the shape of an arrow. Etched on one side of the bag were the words: "To Mrs. Lawson from Mary Bartel." Just the sight of it brought a lump to Sophie's throat.

Sophie deliberately waited until the end to open Mary's package. Each time she had reached for it, she pulled back, fearing whatever was in the sack might be so cheap that Mary would be embarrassed. Saving it for last, Sophie hoped by moving quickly she could minimize the damage.

Taking the white sack in hand and giving it a shake, Sophie said, "Last but not least, this one is from Mary."

"Nice wrapping paper!" Curtis Shepherd blurted out, then ducked behind the boy in front of him.

Sophie smiled and admired the outside of the package. "You're right, Curtis," she agreed, holding it up for the others to see. "It looks like Mary went to a lot of work to make this extra special."

Then she carefully pulled off the tape and reached into the bag. Inside was an object lightly wrapped in

a kitchen paper towel, and Sophie opened it, unveil-
ing a cheap black plastic watch with a digital dial
that showed the dull scratches of many years of wear.

The smirks that broke out across Mrs. Lawson's
class quickly turned to giggles. But Sophie immedi-
ately silenced them by exclaiming, "I can't believe it.
This is just what I've needed all year. I'm so tired of
winding this old watch I've been wearing. This one
runs by batteries, doesn't it?"

Mary nodded and smiled.

"Wonderful!" Taking off the expensive watch her
husband had given her on their tenth wedding
anniversary, Sophie strapped on the black plastic
watch and admired it. "Look! It even has the date on
it. Now I have no excuse for not knowing what day it
is! Thank you so much, Mary. It fits perfectly."

Some of the children were surprised at first by
Sophie's response, but most became caught up in
their teacher's excitement. Sophie saw Anne put her
arm around Mary and whisper her congratulations.
Mary was clearly the unlikely winner for having

brought the best gift on this cold winter's day.

At the close of the day, as the boys and girls exited the room, Mary dawdled at her desk until the last student was gone. Then she picked up her schoolbag and slowly approached Sophie, who was seated at her desk.

"Mary," Sophie said, "my husband and I are heading out of town for a special birthday dinner, so there's no work after school today. We'll start again next week. Besides, you deserve a Valentine's break for all the hard effort you've been giving. I'm so pleased with your progress."

"Thank you, Mrs. Lawson," Mary replied softly. "But I'm not here about my schoolwork."

"What is it, Mary? Is everything okay?"

For the first time since joining Sophie's class, Mary's brown eyes filled with tears and she began to cry. Sophie reached out and took Mary into her arms, holding her tightly as the little girl shook and sobbed. It may have been five minutes, it may have been fifteen, but Sophie simply let Mary cry until the well of tears was empty and she was calm again.

Still hugging her, Sophie whispered, "It's okay to cry, sweetheart. Did someone say something about your gift that hurt you?"

Mary shook her head no but did not speak.

"So, what's wrong, Mary?" asked Sophie soothingly. "Was it me?"

First came a shaking no, then Mary nodded.

"What did I do?"

Pulling away and looking into Sophie's eyes, Mary answered quietly, "I'm so happy you like my gift, Mrs. Lawson. It was my mother's, and it looks good on you."

"Dear Lord Jesus!" Sophie gasped, taking Mary back into her embrace and squeezing her tightly. While tears streaked down the faces of both teacher and student, something deep inside Sophie's heart broke for this poor little bird whose wings she sought to heal. This time it was the young girl who waited for her teacher's tears to end.

"Ohhh!" sighed Sophie, taking a deep draught of

air after she dried her tears. "Mary, your mother's watch is the finest present I could ever hope to receive, and I promise I will wear it with pride. I feel very honored that you would give me something so precious to you."

Mary stood up and smiled warmly at Sophie, although her lovely eyes still wore their sadness. "Grandmother thought it was a good idea," she whispered. "She said you'd like it, and she hoped it would make you feel like we felt at Christmas. Happy Valentine's, Mrs. Lawson."

"Happy Valentine's to you, dear Mary." Choking up once again, Sophie took Mary's slender hand in her own. "And I promise you by the end of the school year you'll be ready for seventh grade. In fact, you'll do great!"

"I couldn't do it without your help," Mary said. Then she kissed Sophie on the cheek and gave her another hug before leaving.

Sitting alone in the utter silence of her class-room, Sophie Lawson bowed her head and thanked

God for that "something more" He had put in her
heart. The Father who had given His own Son to
die for the sins of the world had also placed His love
deep inside her heart, and that, she knew, was a
miracle.

Is not this the kind of fasting I have chosen: to loose the chains of injustice and untie the cords of the yoke, to set the oppressed free and break every yoke? Is it not to share your food with the hungry and to provide the poor wanderer with shelter—when you see the naked, to clothe him, and not to turn away from your own flesh and blood? Then your light will break forth like the dawn, and your healing will quickly appear; then your righteousness will go before you, and the glory of the Lord will be your rear guard.

Isaiah 58:6–8

*I*t was mid-April before the last vestiges of the snowy Minnesota winter were driven back and spring brought its welcome southerly breezes, transforming the rural countryside from dull browns and grays to a wonderful array of green grasses and flowers in every hue imaginable.

Sophie was standing by the classroom window, admiring a cluster of apple trees whose luscious white blossoms had seemingly exploded overnight. In contrast to the dry, stale air of the winter months, a refreshing fragrance had filled her room throughout the day, and she was tempted to leave the window open for the night. With a measure of resignation, she took the window crank and turned it slowly as she prepared to leave for the day.

A soft knock at the classroom door startled Sophie, and she jumped as she turned from the window. Caught off guard, she was surprised to see that her visitor was Mary Bartel's grandmother.

"Whew!" Sophie gasped and smiled at Mildred Jacobsen. "I was daydreaming out the window. Please pardon my reaction, and do come in."

Mrs. Jacobsen returned Sophie's smile as she entered the room. "I should have waited to knock until you'd turned around. Didn't mean to frighten you."

Sophie thought Mary's grandmother to be in her mid-fifties, but it was difficult to tell. Her short, curly hair was dyed black, and her outdated plastic glasses sat crooked on her plump face. In her work uniform, her short, stocky frame appeared hunched and tired.

"I'm sorry I've come so late," Mrs. Jacobsen apologized, looking a bit frazzled, "but I was trying to clear up some trouble at work. Do you have a minute?"

"Certainly," replied Sophie, walking to her desk and pointing to the extra chair. "How can I help you, Mrs. Jacobsen?"

Mary's grandmother smiled and sat down beside

Sophie. "Oh, my! You've already helped me enough for an entire lifetime, Mrs. Lawson. I've not come today for more help."

There was a pause, and finally Sophie said, "I'm sorry, I don't know what you mean."

"I think you do," suggested Mrs. Jacobsen with a nod. "You're the one who's helped change Mary's life."

Sophie was puzzled and shifted in her chair to face Mary's grandmother squarely. "I'm still not sure what you mean, Mrs. Jacobsen. If it's about Mary's progress in school, be assured, Mary's the one who should get the credit. She's worked harder than any student I've ever seen."

"I'd be pleased if you'd call me Millie," the older woman said, pushing her glasses back up on her nose. "That's what my friends call me. And you're more than a friend to Mary and me."

"Millie," Sophie responded. "I'm delighted you consider me a friend. Your little Mary has become one of the great joys in my life. She's a wonderful girl."

Mildred Jacobsen's eyes filled with a sudden rush of tears, and her face flushed from its usual pale to a bright red. She looked away from Sophie and shut her eyes for a few seconds, then reached up and rubbed her forehead. Finally she shook her head and smiled again. "I didn't come to cry today, Mrs. Lawson, but I've come to offer my poor thanks for the great debt I owe you. It's a bill I'm overdue on; I should have come sooner."

Sophie still wasn't sure why Mary's grandmother had come, so she waited for her to explain.

"What you've done for Mary academically, I can't possibly give you enough praise," Mildred began, brushing aside a few loose tears. "Back last summer when I got the call from my daughter, Mary's aunt Beth, saying that with her own family to raise she couldn't take care of Mary, I really didn't know what I was going to do. Since she was small, Mary was as backward as they come. I was told she'd never amount to nothing in school. You pulled her—"

"I just did what any teacher—"

"No," Mary's grandmother broke in. "You did what no teacher has done, and probably what no other teacher ever would have done. Mary's mother went through school and struggled just like her, but no one took any more interest in her than a stick. Things might be different today if someone had. But you've given Mary a chance, and she's not the same little girl who moved in with me back in August, Mrs. Lawson. I thought she was hopeless."

Choking up, Sophie looked intently into Mrs. Jacobsen's eyes and simply nodded. "I understand," she whispered.

"But you've done more than that for Mary," Mildred continued, "and that's the part I don't understand. You've somehow made Mary feel you love her, and that's made all the difference. I'm not sure Mary has ever felt loved before—even by her mother, or by me. Why do you love her as you do?"

Sophie shrugged her shoulders and didn't know what to say. "You shouldn't compare me with Mary's mother or with—"

"Mrs. Lawson," Mary's grandmother interjected, "I'm not here meaning to compare. I'm here to discover what makes you love all your students as you do, not just Mary. The fact is, my daughter and I both have failed to give Mary the love she's needed. It's too late for my daughter, but it's not too late for me. Christmas was proof of that. Can you help me?"

"My goodness," whispered Sophie, overwhelmed by Mildred Jacobsen's sincerity. "I can only tell you what has made a difference in my life, but you may find it offensive."

"I work in a rest home, Mrs. Lawson. *Offensive* is a word I live with."

Taking a deep breath, Sophie asked, "Do you mind my asking if you go to church, Millie?"

"Not at all," Mildred responded. "I haven't gone since I was a teenager. Occasionally I make it into a church for a wedding or funeral."

"Do you believe in God?"

"I guess I do," she answered. "What difference does it make?"

"For me, it's made all the difference in the world," Sophie replied. "Do you remember the night Mary tried to sing her solo?"

"Yes."

"That was the night it came to me very clearly that though I tried to show equal care for all my students, the fact was, I didn't really love the ones like Mary as God wanted me to. I saw how inadequate my love was for the boys and girls who needed me most. So I asked God to do whatever it took to put His love inside me. And it started with Mary. It was as if my heart had to be broken so God could give me the love those students needed. I don't know how else to explain it."

Quietly staring into space, Mary's grandmother thought over what Sophie had said. "I'd like to believe you, Mrs. Lawson, and I don't mind you talking about religion, but it sounds a bit strange to me. If I wanted to look into it for myself, where would I start?"

Sophie smiled warmly and answered, "Well, for

starters, you and Mary could consider coming to
church with my husband and me. I think you'll
discover a whole group of people who have the love
that I'm talking about."

Mildred Jacobsen raised her eyebrows and shook
her head. "You don't want to be seen with me, Mrs.
Lawson. I got a bad reputation in this community,
and truth is, I earned it. I'll be happy to come, but
I'm not about to shame you folks."

"Oh no!" Sophie exclaimed, putting her hand on
Mildred's arm. "If you go, you're coming with us.
Didn't you say we're friends?"

Mildred smiled and nodded, "But..."

"No *buts*!" admonished Sophie. "We'd really like
to have you come to church with us, Millie, but why
don't you first think over the things we've discussed
and talk a bit with Mary. Then I'll call to see what
you've decided."

"I'd like to do that," Mildred agreed.

Opening her desk drawer, Sophie asked, "Do you
have a Bible, Millie?"

"No," she answered, looking perplexed. "Do you have to have one to get in?"

"No, no," replied Sophie, shaking her head as she pulled a paperback Bible from the drawer. "But I'm getting ahead of myself. Church is one place where I believe you'll discover the truth of what I've said. Another place is in the Bible. If I give you a copy, would you read it?"

"I'll try," Mildred answered, "but I'm a mighty poor reader."

"You could have Mary read it to you," Sophie suggested. "Then both of you can discover what the Bible teaches."

"I like that," Mary's grandmother said. "We could learn together."

"That's the best way!" Handing Mildred the Bible, Sophie said,

"Please take it."

"Oh no, I can't," Mrs. Jacobsen muttered. "I'll get one—"

"Look at it," Sophie interrupted. "I've used it for years, and it didn't cost much when I got it. I want you to have it. Besides, I have more at home that aren't being used."

Mildred took the well-worn Bible and held it carefully in her hands. "Thank you so much, Mrs. Lawson. We'll give it a try." She opened the book and gently turned over the pages. "It seems pretty big. Do we start at the beginning?"

"Here," Sophie said, taking the Bible and picking up a loose paper from her desk. "Start right here in the gospel of John where I'm placing this marker, and I promise that you and Mary will learn about the love God has for each of you, and the love you can have for others." With that, Sophie placed the Bible back in Millie's hands.

As Mildred looked down at the Bible, a troubled frown crossed her brow. She lifted her eyes to Sophie and asked, "Is there anything else I can do for Mary, Mrs. Lawson?"

Sophie nodded, but was surprised to discover a lump in her throat and tears clustering in the corners of her eyes. It took a bit of doing, but she finally found the words. "Have you ever taken Mary into your arms and told her you love her?"

Mildred's lower lip trembled, and she began to cry softly. "No, I can't even..."

As her words trailed off, Sophie squeezed Mrs. Jacobsen's hand. "This is your chance, Millie. Do it first thing when you get home today, and do it again every day. There's no one else in the world who can give Mary a grandmother's love. Don't let anything cheat Mary out of your love."

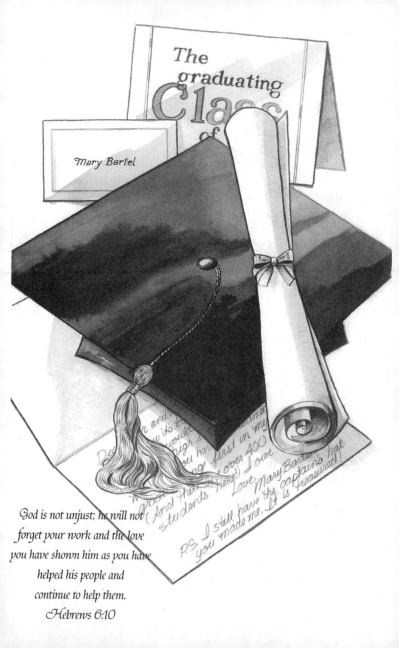

The graduating **Class** of

Mary Bartel

God is not unjust; he will not forget your work and the love you have shown him as you have helped his people and continue to help them.
Hebrews 6:10

*A*ll too soon the school year came to a close, and Sophie Lawson found herself giving hugs and wishing her students the very best in the future as they exited her sixth-grade classroom for the last time. It was especially hard to say goodbye to Mary Bartel, although Sophie knew she would see her special student every Sunday in church with her grandmother. By the end of the most amazing year of Sophie's teaching career, Mary had caught up with most of the students and was even ahead of many others in math and science.

The following year, Mary's grandmother hurt her back while helping lift an elderly woman in the rest home and the injury put her out of work. Although there was some disability coverage and many people in the church pitched in to help them financially, as soon as Mary finished seventh grade, she and her grandmother sadly packed their meager belongings and moved to St. Louis to live with Mrs. Jacobsen's elderly bachelor brother. His health was failing, and by caring for him they were insured a roof over their heads.

The first year they were gone, Sophie heard from Mary and her grandmother a few times. But once they settled into their new lives in St. Louis, they didn't write for several years. Then one day in May, Sophie received a high school graduation announcement and a short note that read:

Dear Mr. and Mrs. Lawson,

I know it's too far for you to come, but I would love to have you come to my high school graduation ceremony. Would you ever have dreamed that I'm graduating first in my class? (And there are over four hundred students here!) I owe it all to you.

Love,
Mary Bartel

P.S. I still have the captain's hat you made me. It is treasured!

Although she truly wished she could go, a trip to
St. Louis was out of the question for Sophie. She did
call to congratulate Mary on the evening of her
graduation and was amazed at how articulate and
confident her once painfully backward little Mary
had become. Mrs. Jacobsen's brother had passed
away during the previous year and left Mildred the
house and enough money for her and Mary to live
comfortably.

Four years passed by, and then came a phone call
late one evening.

"Mrs. Lawson," said a quiet voice. "This is Mary
Bartel."

"Mary!" cried Sophie. "It's so good to hear your
voice. How are you doing?"

"I'm fine, Mrs. Lawson," Mary replied. "Actually,
I'm doing wonderfully. I've called to tell you that I
finally made it through nursing school and they've
asked me to speak at our graduation!"

"Congratulations!" exclaimed Sophie. "I'm sure
you'll make a fantastic nurse."

"I've already got a job and can hardly wait to start," said Mary. "I love it!"

"We'd love to come for the graduation," Sophie added. "When is it?"

There was a pause on the other end of the line, then Mary slowly responded, "I'd be delighted if you and Mr. Lawson could make it to the graduation, but I have a bigger request of you."

"What is it, Mary?"

"On the twelfth of June," Mary's voice got softer, "I'm getting married, and I'd like the two of you to come and sit where my grandmother would have sat. She died this spring."

"Oh, Mary, I'm so sorry," Sophie sympathized.

"Thank you, Mrs. Lawson. Before Grandmother passed away, she suggested I ask Mr. Lawson to give me away if he would. Grandmother would be very proud."

Nothing could have kept Bill and Sophie Lawson from attending that wedding. They arrived the day before the ceremony, giving Sophie and Mary time

You are
cordially invited
to the
wedding
of
Mary Bartel
to
John Pe

12ᵗʰ of June
at
First Chu
St. l
Re

to reminisce and fill in the missing years. They laughed and cried as they shared their stories of what they had experienced together and what had happened since parting. Neither Bill nor Sophie could believe that Mary, now a lovely, radiant bride-to-be, had once been that wounded, expressionless little bird in the third row of Sophie's sixth-grade class.

As Sophie was ushered down the long church aisle to the front pew on the bride's side, her thoughts were arrested by the memory of the simple dream she had had about Mary so many years before. Four simple words to a plain little girl—"I love you, Mary"—had not only made a difference in Mary's life, but Sophie knew they had changed her life as well. And now, as the wonderful memories changed to tears, Sophie prayed for one more opportunity to do something special for Mary.

The organist began playing the processional, and Sophie watched the proud groom and his attendants step from the back of the church and take their places. One by one, Mary's lovely bridesmaids came forward and were escorted to their positions on the platform. Then everyone stood as Mary came forward on Bill Lawson's strong arm, looking as beautiful as any bride Sophie had ever seen. "Oh, Mary, little Mary," she whispered.

When Mary and Bill got to the front pews, Mary stopped to give Sophie a hug and kiss, and something inside Sophie told her this was the moment she had prayed for. Putting her arms around Mary and hugging her tightly, Sophie whispered in her ear, "I have a present I want to give you now, Mary."

Mary looked surprised but held out her hand as Sophie handed her something wrapped in a kitchen paper towel. Sophie said softly, "I've worn it to my classroom every day since you gave it to me, and now it's time for you to have it."

Pulling off the paper, Mary gave a delighted gasp. Ever so slowly, she held it up into the shimmering candlelight and for a moment seemed to step back in time and space. An anxious organist looked over the organ to see what was delaying the bride and had no choice but to repeat the melody again.

Those gathered for the wedding had no idea why Mary was holding up a cheap old broken watch, but Mary's expression left no doubt that to her it was priceless. Surprising everyone, she handed Sophie her bouquet of flowers and fastened the watch on her wrist. Her task complete, Mary looked into Sophie's eyes but could not speak her thanks.

Tears were pouring down Sophie's face, but she managed to say, "Remember, the world changes—one person at a time. So wear it proudly, dear Mary. The future belongs to you."

The organ music swelled and a radiant Mary took her bouquet from Sophie and stepped forward to meet her groom.